The GREAT SANTA CLAUS MYSTERY

Written by Fran and Lou Sabin

Illustrated by Irene Trivas

Troll Associates

Library of Congress Cataloging in Publication Data

Sabin, Francene.
   The great Santa Claus mystery.

   (A Troll easy-to-read mystery)
   Summary: While on a Christmas shopping trip,
the Maple Street Six become involved in a frantic
search for a sneaky Santa.
   [1. Santa Claus—Fiction. 2. Mystery and detec-
tive stories. 3. Christmas stories] I. Sabin,
Louis. II. Trivas, Irene, ill. III. Title.
IV. Series: Troll easy-to-read mystery.
PZ7.S1172Gs   [Fic]   81-7530
ISBN 0-89375-602-4 (case)   AACR2
ISBN 0-89375-603-2 (pbk.)

10   9   8   7   6   5   4   3   2

The GREAT SANTA CLAUS MYSTERY

Eddie

Sam

Sue

Annie

Sarah

Mike

the Maple Street Six

Everyone in the Maple Street Six likes Christmas.

Sue likes the bright lights.

Mike likes the music.

Eddie likes making strings of popcorn for the tree.

Annie likes making lists to send to Santa.

Sam likes the turkey, stuffing, mince pie, and gingerbread cookies.

I like Christmas shopping most of all. My name is Sarah. I am president of our club.

This year we all went shopping together. The stores were crowded and noisy and exciting. There were cars and trucks honking their horns. There were people carrying big boxes. They were rushing in and out of stores. There was a band playing Christmas songs.

And on every corner, there was a
Santa. There was a tall Santa with very
big feet, and a short one with glasses on
the tip of his red nose. One Santa rang his
bell as hard and fast as he could. The one
we liked the best was fat and had a merry,
booming laugh. When he said, "Ho! Ho!
Ho!" we all felt happy.

"Let's go to the toy department first,"
said Eddie.

"No," said Mike. "I want to buy a
Christmas card."

Sue shook her head. "I want to talk to
the store Santa. I have a long list for
him."

"I am so-o-o hungry," said Sam.
"Can't we eat now? Please?"

"Toys first," said Eddie.

"Santa first," said Sue.

"Food first," Sam begged.

"First, stop fighting," Annie said, "so we can take a vote."

The vote came out to be cards first, then toys, then Santa, then lunch.

Sam was sad.

He dug into his pocket and pulled out a cookie. "I guess I'll have to get by with this," he sighed.

"Don't worry," Mike laughed. "We won't let you starve."

There were rows and rows of cards. There were Christmas cards and birthday cards, friendship cards and get-well cards. There were cards for every kind of day you could think of.

"Hey, everybody," Mike said. "Help me. I need a card for my parents."

"Okay," we said. We each went in a different direction.

"I found a perfect one," Annie called out a few minutes later. She read it out loud.

"Season's greetings, Mom and Dad,
From a son who loves you both
like mad!"

Mike clapped his hands. "Wow! That's just what I wanted."

Mike paid for the card. Then we headed for the toy department.

Right in the middle of the store we saw a large crowd of people. We squeezed through to see what was so exciting.

"Whew!" Sue whistled softly. "Look at that."

There was a round table. In the
middle was a doll-sized black sled. In
front of the sled were eight gold reindeer.
Next to the sled was a Christmas tree
about twelve inches tall. It had rubies and
emeralds hanging on it. The rubies were
a very dark red. The emeralds were a
very bright green. And sprinkled over
everything was silver sparkle dust.

Sue moved closer to the table. "That is the most beautiful thing I ever saw," she said.

"I'll get it for you. Just say the word," Mike said. He stepped up to the table. He had a big grin on his face.

"Stop right where you are, young man," a voice growled. It was a man in uniform. He was guarding the things on the table.

"Gee, mister. He was just joking," Sam said.

"Well, we can't take any chances," the guard said. "There are desperate criminals who would stop at nothing to steal all this. Maybe one of them is disguised as a young boy, like your friend here."

"Me?" Mike asked. "A desperate criminal?"

Annie grinned. "I always knew they'd catch up with you, Mike," she said.

"If the police put you in jail, I'll bring you a cake," Sam added.

Mike looked afraid. "No more jokes, gang," I said. Then I told the guard that Mike is a very honest person.

"I'm sure he is," the guard said. He smiled. "I was just teasing."

I grabbed Mike's hand, and we all hurried off to see the toys.

What a toy department! Millions of
stuffed animals and games and dolls and
trains were everywhere.

Eddie walked over to a counter. He
picked up a shiny whistle. "That's it," he
said. "Just what Joey wants. He likes to
play policeman."

Joey is Eddie's little brother. He is three years old. He is a real pest.

Eddie paid for the whistle. "Shall I gift wrap it?" the clerk asked.

"No, thanks," Eddie answered. "I'll do it at home."

"Okay, that's done. Can we have lunch now?" Sam asked.

"I want to play with the trains first," said Sue.

"I want to try that dart board," said Mike.

Annie wanted to see the stuffed animals. Eddie and I wanted to look at the books.

Poor Sam had to wait.

"Come on. It's time to see Santa," Sue said.

"Awww, I want to play some more," grumbled Mike.

"You played for a half hour," Sam said. "If we don't hurry, we won't see Santa. He eats lunch, too."

We followed the signs that said, "TO SANTA." Then we saw his big chair. It was empty.

"Told you so," Sam said. "Santa's out to lunch."

"No, he isn't. He's over there," I said.
Santa was standing behind a post with ribbons around it. We could see just a bit of his red coat and shiny black boots.

"Oh, good! I have my list right here,"
Annie said.

"Me, too," said Sue.

We all ran over to Santa.

He was a strange Santa. He looked angry behind his beard. He didn't say, "Ho! Ho! Ho!" or "Merry Christmas!" He didn't even smile.

"Whatcha want?" he grumbled.

"Before you go to lunch, Santa, would you please listen to my list?" Annie asked politely.

"And mine," said Sue.

"Please," said Mike.

"All right," Santa said. "Just make it quick."

Santa sat on the big chair. "Okay, girlie," he said to Annie. "Let's hear it."

"Don't you want to know if I was good all year?" Annie asked him.

"Yeah. Sure. Were you good?" Santa said.

But he did not look as if he cared at all.

Annie started to read her list. It was a long one. Santa didn't let her finish it.

"Listen, kids," Santa said. "I'm in a hurry. Give me all your lists. I'll read them back at the—heh-heh—North Pole."

He grabbed the lists from our hands. He stuffed them in his pockets and rushed off.

"At last! It's lunch time!" Sam shouted.

It had been a busy morning. Everybody was ready to eat. We walked through the store, past the toy department. Suddenly, we heard a scream, then a lot of yelling and a loud *Thump!* It was coming from the middle of the store—from the place with the beautiful little sled and gold reindeer.

There was a lot of pushing and
shoving going on. Then we saw a Santa
Claus knocking people this way and that.
He swung a sack onto his back and began
to run.

"Stop, thief!" a man called out.
"Police, police!" a woman shrieked.

The guard was on the floor. The thief had knocked him down. The table was empty. The sled and the reindeer and the jewels were gone.

"Don't let him get away!" Eddie
shouted.

We raced through the store. Santa ran
out to the street. We dashed through the
front door—and stopped.

"There he is," said Sam.

"No, *there* he is," Sue said.

"Oh, oh. We have a problem," I
moaned.

"Yeah, a *big* problem," said Eddie.

There was a Santa on every corner.
Two more Santas were crossing the street.
There were Santas everywhere!

"We'll never find him now," Annie said.

"Yes, we will!" I said. "Here's a clue."

I pointed to the sidewalk. Something was glittering there.

"It's sparkle dust. There was lots of it on the table where the sled was," I said.

"Yes, I remember it!" Eddie said.

Sue walked a few steps away. "Look, there's more here," she called out.

I waved my arm. "Come on, gang. We'll get that sneaky Santa!"

There were crowds of shoppers all around. It was hard to find the trail of sparkle dust. But the Maple Street Six never give up.

"Here's more," Sam cried.

There was a shiny patch at the curb. And another in the middle of the road.

"That's him!" Annie yelled. She was staring at a Santa on the other side of the street.

We rushed over to the Santa. He gave us a wide smile. "Merry Christmas! Have you been good?" he asked.

"Yes, but you haven't," Mike said.

"Just hand over the sled and stuff," Annie growled.

Santa looked puzzled. "The whole sled? Then there won't be toys for anyone else."

This wasn't the thief. We could tell that.

"Sorry, we want a different Santa," I said.

"No Santa in the world can give you the whole sled," he said.

We felt silly. We told him about the thief. This Santa was nice. He understood.

"We must find him," Santa said. "In all my years, not one of my helpers ever did such a bad thing."

Sue's eyes opened wide. "One of *your* helpers?" she asked.

Santa smiled. Then he said, "Look! There is the trail of sparkle dust!"

We followed the trail for three blocks. Then our Santa said, "That's the man you want."

He pointed at a Santa standing in a doorway.

"Yes, that's the one," Annie said.

"How can you be sure?" Sam asked.

"There's sparkle dust all over his suit," Annie said.

The thief saw us. He tried to sneak off through the crowd.

"He'll get away!" cried Sue.

"No, he won't," Eddie said.

He took out the whistle he had bought for Joey. *"Breeeeet! Breeeeet! Breeeeet!"* Eddie blew hard on the whistle—again and again.

A police officer came running over.

"He's the Santa who robbed the store," I told her.

The officer grabbed the thief. He tried to get away. He dropped his sack. The sled and the reindeer and the jewels fell out. Then his beard fell off.

"It's Snake-Eyes Sutton! We've been after him for a long time. And you kids caught him," said the officer.

"This nice Santa helped us," I said.

"What nice Santa is that?" asked the police officer.

We looked around. The jolly Santa Claus was gone.

"He vanished like magic," Sue said.

"Like he was the real Santa Claus," Eddie said.

"Do you think we'll ever see him
again?" Annie asked.

"I hope so," said Sue.

"Let's go look for him," Mike said.

"No! Let's have lunch," Sam shouted.
"PLEASE!"

And that's just what we did.